WITHDRAWN

TO SOSI AND ILA, MAY YOUR DREAMS ALWAYS BE FLEEPY.

Acknowledgements:
I wish to thank lovely Kallie and Tiffany for all their hard work and great ideas.
This book would never have happened without them. —L. J. S.

Published in 2014 by Simply Read Books www.simplyreadbooks.com
Text & illustrations © 2014 Lori Joy Smith

Library and Archives Canada Cataloguing in Publication

Smith, Lori Joy, 1973-, author, illustrator
The goodnight book / written and illustrated by Lori Joy Smith.
ISBN 978-1-927018-42-2 (bound)
I. Title.
PS8637.M56523G66 2014   jC813'.6   C2013-906052-9

We gratefully acknowledge for their financial support of our publishing program the Canada Council
for the Arts, the BC Arts Council, and the Government of Canada through the Canada Book Fund
(CBF).

Manufactured in Malaysia.
Book design by Sara Gillingham Studio.

10 9 8 7 6 5 4 3 2 1

LORI JOY SMITH

the GOODNiGHT BOOK

SIMPLY READ BOOKS

In English,
they say

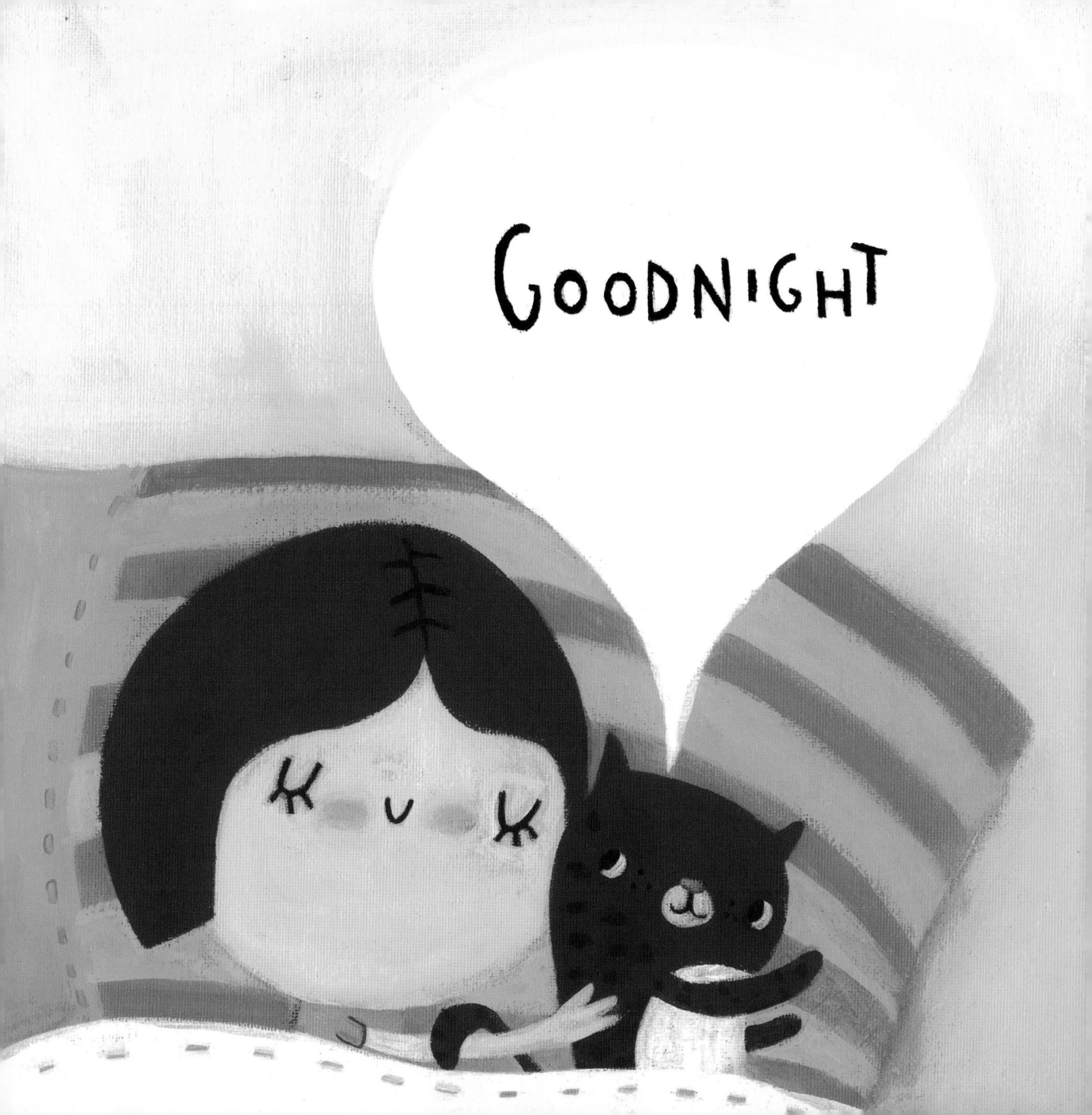
GOODNIGHT

In French,
they say

In Spanish,
they say

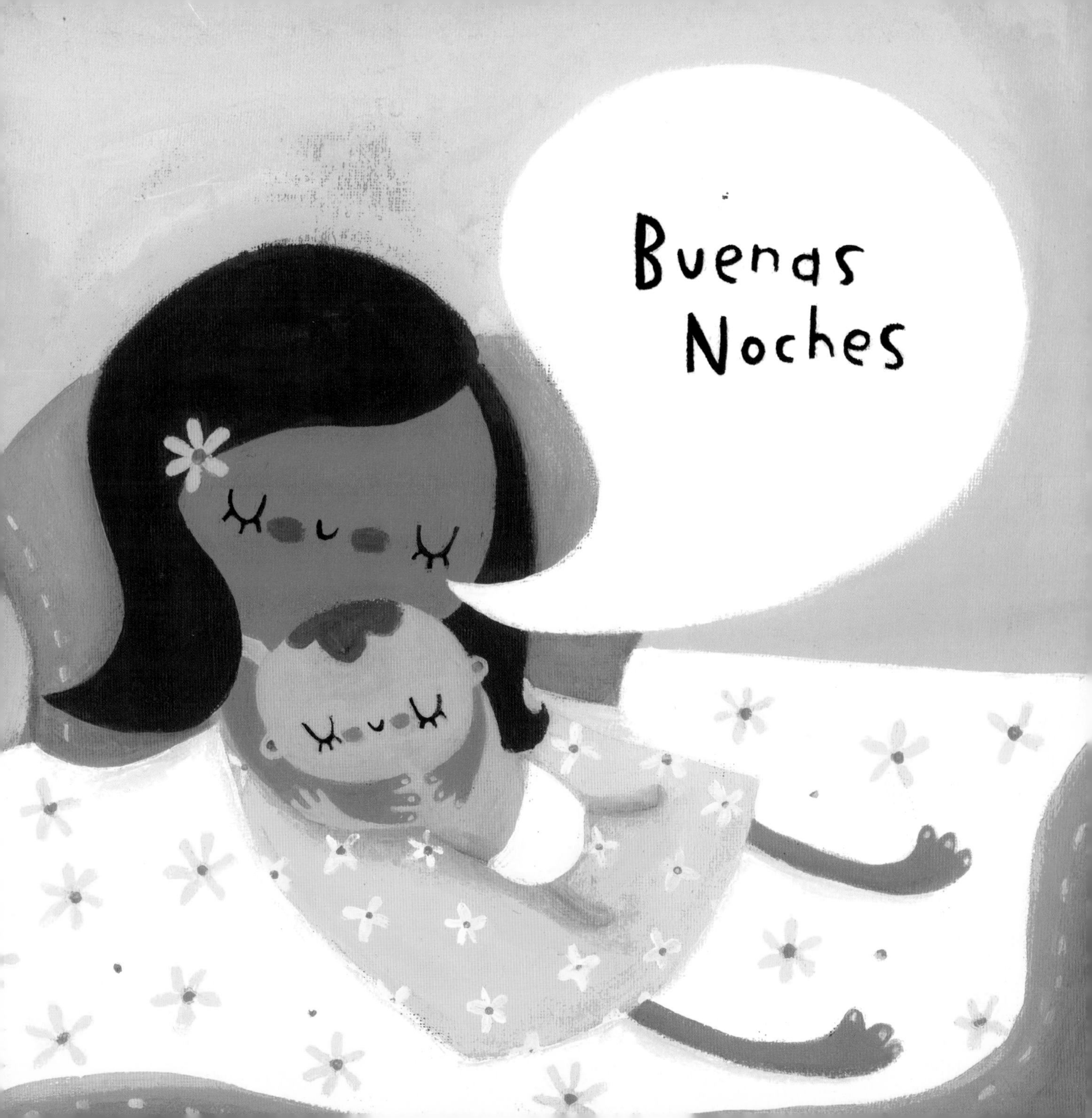
Buenas Noches

But in some far off places they say...

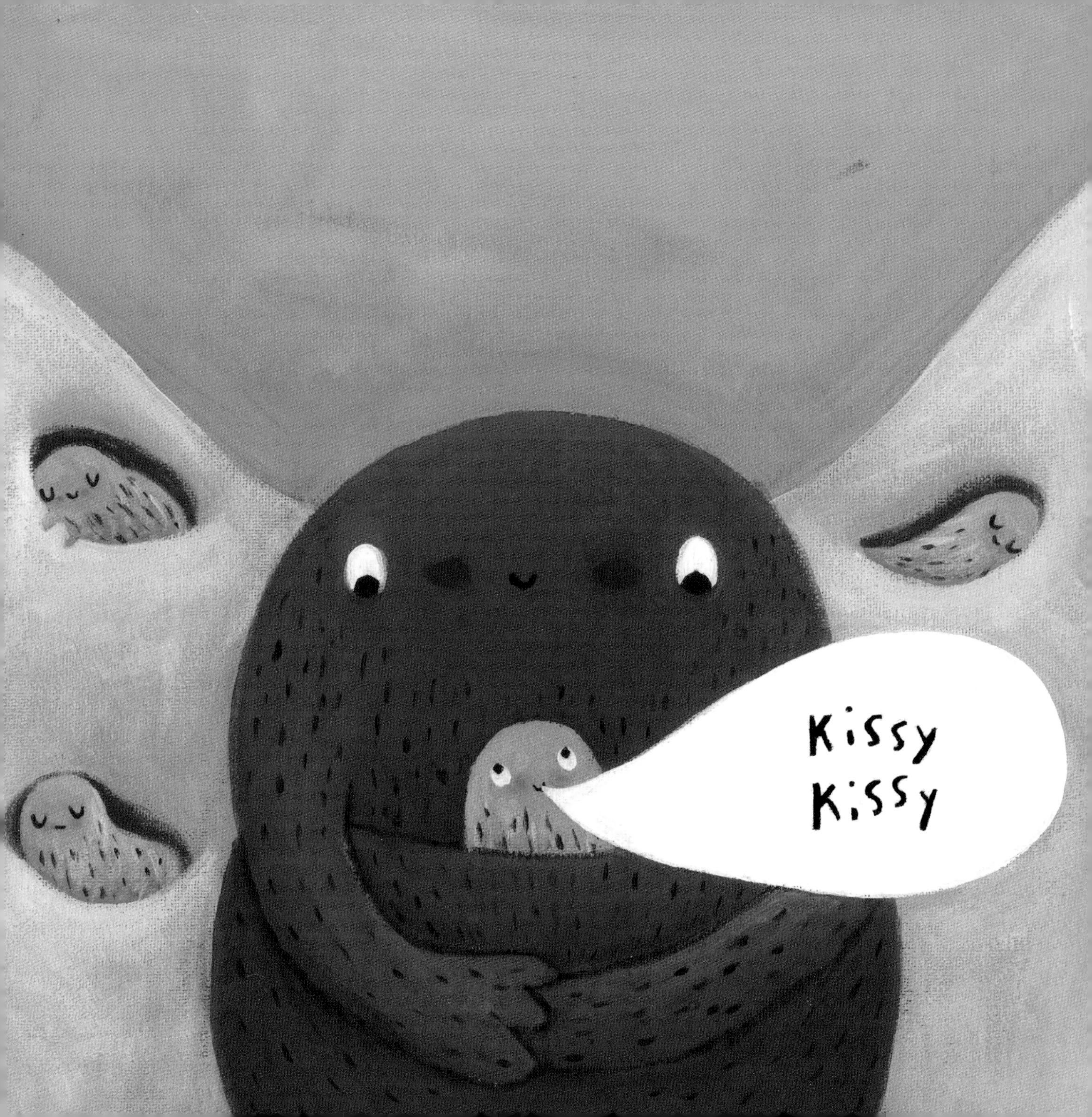
Kissy Kissy

FLEEP
DREAMS

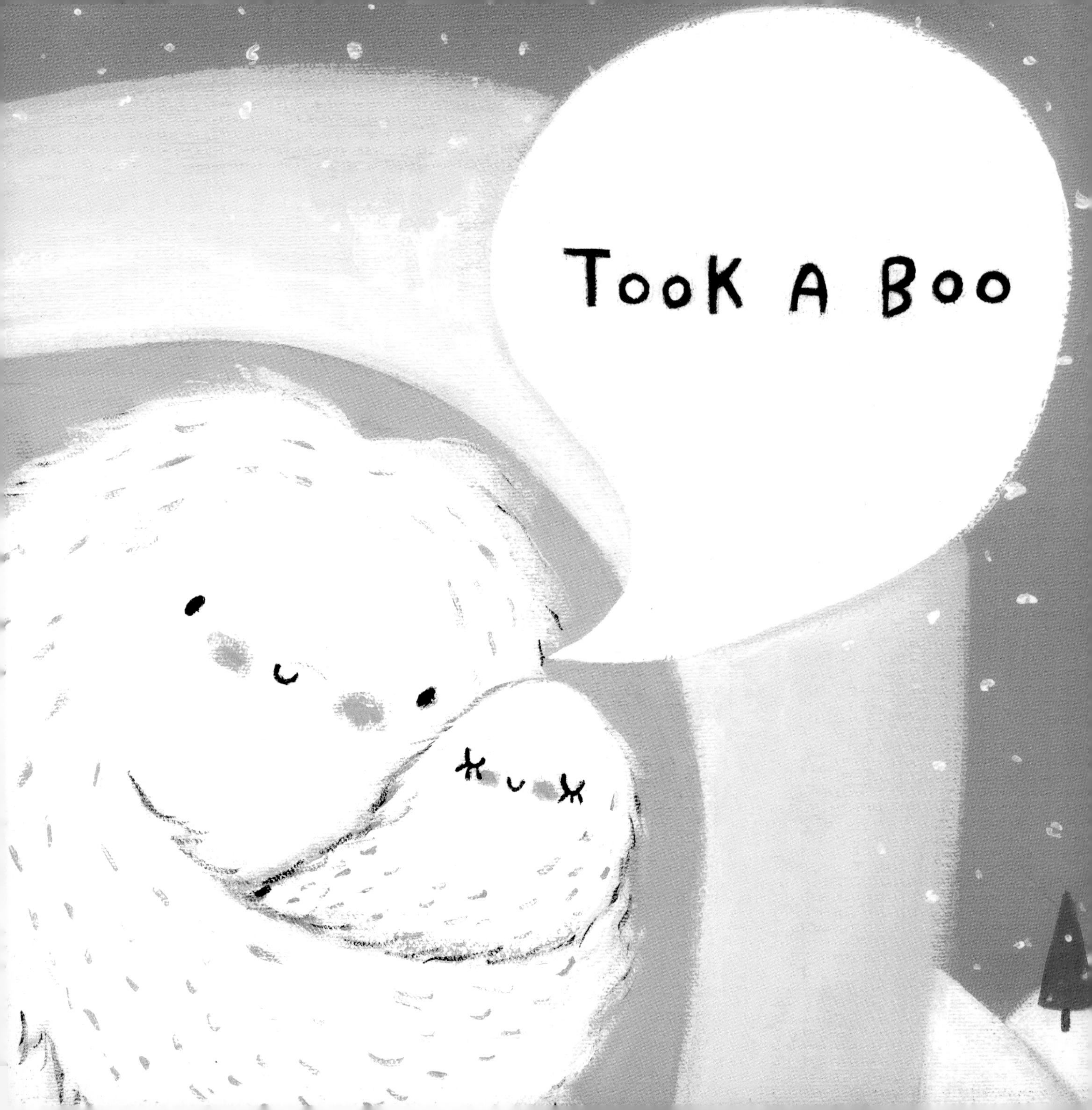
TooK A Boo

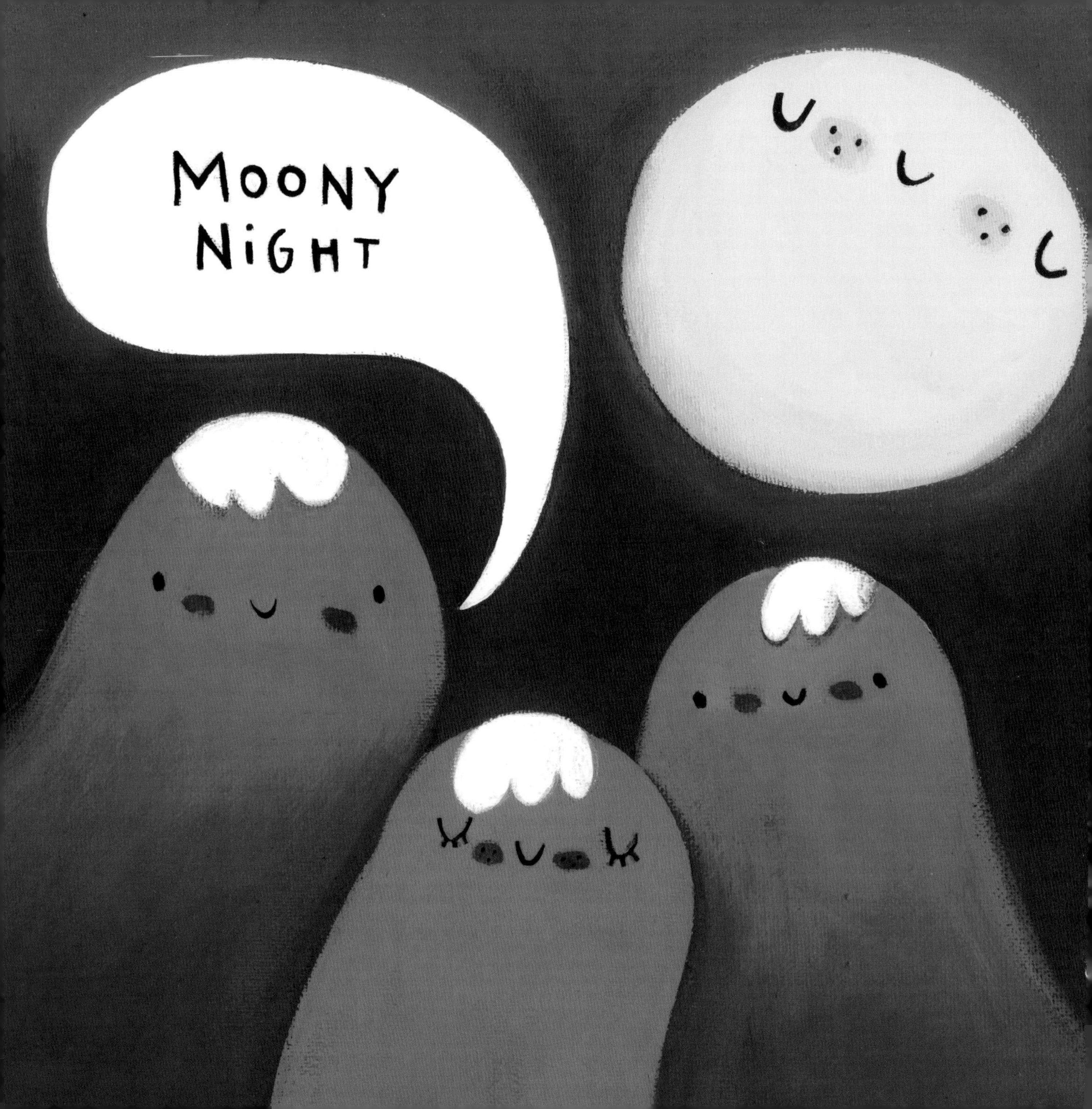
MOONY NIGHT

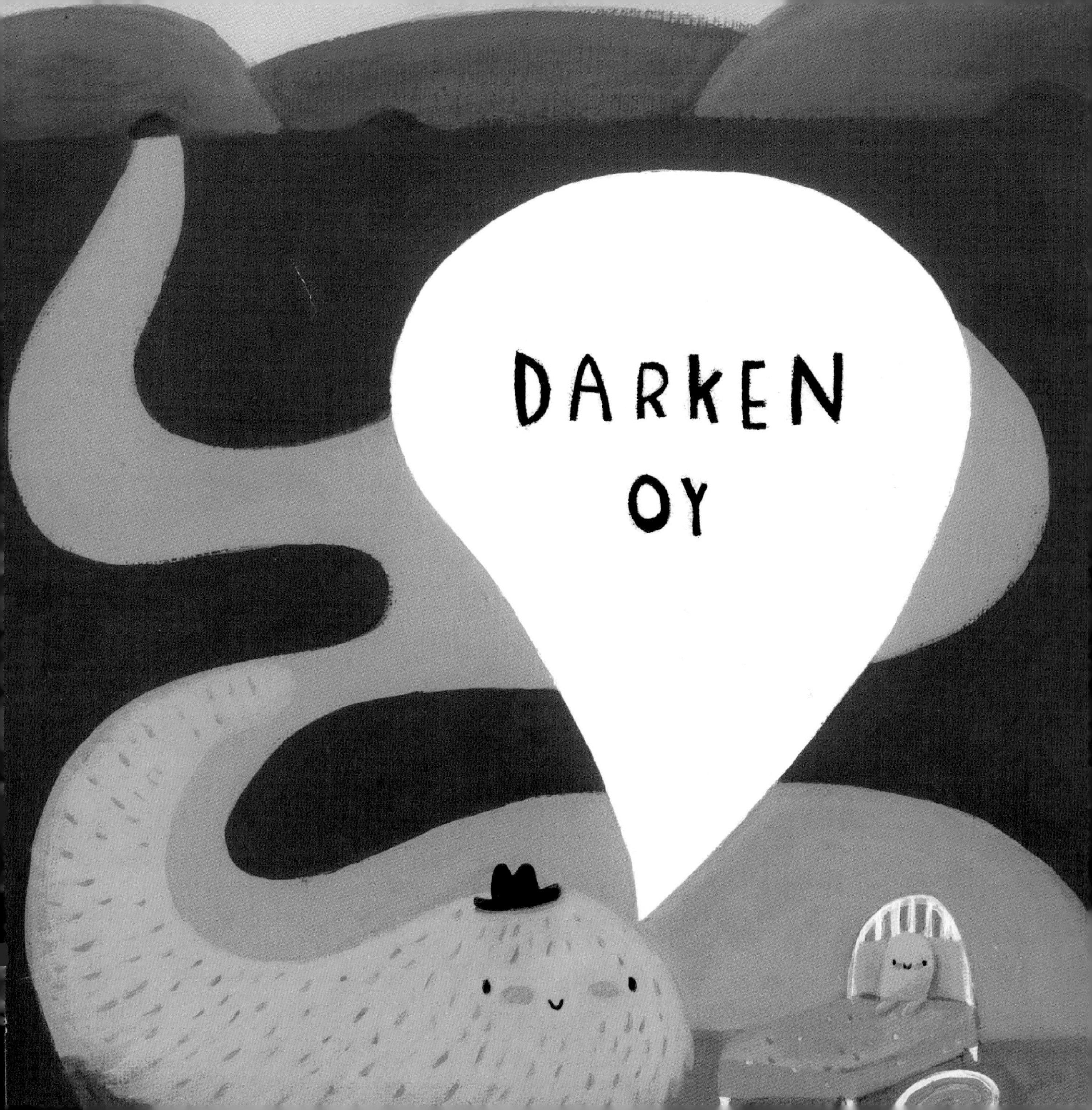
DARKEN
OY

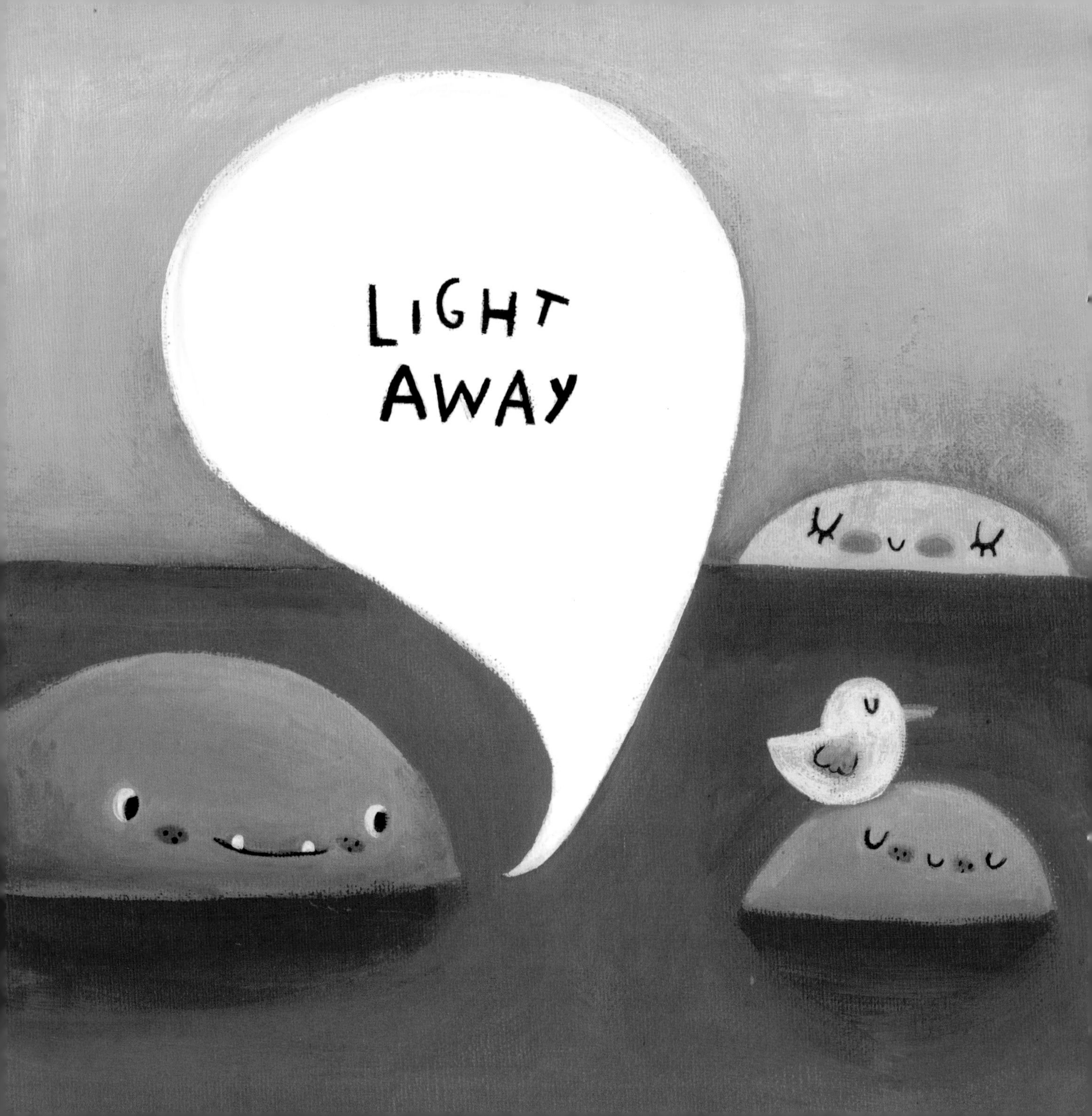
LIGHT AWAY

How do you say GOODNIGHT?